For Bethany, my carbivore. —SVJ

For Hailey, Chris, and my favorite
reformed fussy eater, Brigette. —MR

Text © 2020 by Shelly Vaughan James
Illustrations © 2020 by Matthew Rivera
Cover and internal design © 2020 by Sourcebooks
Internal images © Shutterstock

Watercolors and digital tools were used to create the full-color art.

Published by Sourcebooks Jabberwocky, an imprint of Sourcebooks Kids
P.O. Box 4410, Naperville, Illinois 60567-4410
(630) 961-3900
sourcebookskids.com

Library of Congress Cataloging-in-Publication Data is on file with the publisher.

Source of Production: Leo Paper, Heshan City, Guangdong Province, China
Date of Production: July 2021
Run Number: 5022944

Printed and bound in China.
LEO 10 9 8 7 6 5 4

FUSSY FLAMINGO

WORDS BY
SHELLY VAUGHAN JAMES

PiCTURES BY
MATTHEW RiVERA

sourcebooks
jabberwocky

Mami's neck curves gracefully this morning.

"Your feathers will color soon, Lola."

Papi struts with a kick in his step.

"Eat your fill of shrimp."

When Mami and Papi turn their backs to wade to deeper waters, Lola sticks out her tongue.

Lola dillies on her right leg.

Lola dallies on her left leg.

She dips her black-tipped beak into the water.

But when no one notices,
Lola slips away.

She dawdles below trees
heavy with berries and
sidesteps a falling fruit.

Lola lingers at the shattered shell.

"*¡Ay de mí!*" Mami cries.

"What did you eat?"
Papi asks.

Lola chirps, "I ate creamy **AVOCADO**."

"Please eat shrimp," Papi presses. "Shrimp give your feathers a healthy blush."

The next morning, Mami squawks, "I'm so hungry."

She scoops up shrimp.

Papi hollers, "Oh, me too!" He plops his beak into the water. "Shrimp taste so yummy!"

"Shrimp are soggy,"

sulks Lola.

Mami and Papi wade to deeper waters,
though they swing their necks back over
their wings to watch Lola.

Lola dillies on her right leg.

Lola dallies on her left leg.

She dips her black-tipped beak
into the water.

But when no one notices,
Lola slips away.

She dawdles among evergreen shrubs dotted with pretty globes.

Lola lingers at the bright fruits.

"*¡Ay de mí!*" Mami cries.

"What did you eat?" Papi asks.

Lola chirps, "I ate sweet **PEPiNO MELONS**."

"Please eat shrimp," Mami urges.

"Shrimp help your eyes see far."

The next morning, Papi flaps his feet
to stir up the mucky bottom.

Mami slurps shrimp from the murky water. "Shrimp taste so yummy!"

"Shrimp are muddy," mopes Lola.

Mami and Papi inch ever so slowly toward deeper waters.

Lola dillies on her right leg.

Lola dallies on her left leg.

She dips her black-tipped
beak into the water.

Papi and Mami keep their
eyes peeled.

The day grows nearly dark.
But when no one notices,
Lola slips away.

She dawdles along a pebbly path and spies flowers blooming in a moonbeam.

Lola lingers at the scaly bulbs.

"*¡Ay de mí!*" Mami cries.

"What did you eat?" Papi asks.

Lola chirps, "I ate juicy **DRAGON FRUiTS**."

"Please eat shrimp," Papi pleads. "Shrimp make your wings strong for flying."

The next morning, Mami
begs Lola to eat just one bite.
"Shrimp are yummy."

"Shrimp are yucky."
Lola puckers.

"Have you tried shrimp?" Papi asks.
Lola pouts. "No."

"How do you know you don't like shrimp?" Mami asks.

"I guess," Lola shilly-shallies,

"I could *try* shrimp."

Lola lolls along the shoreline.

Lola dillies on her right leg.

Lola dallies on her left leg.

She dips her black-tipped beak into the water
and sweeps up one ever-so-small shrimp.

She snaps up the shrimp.

Lola **LOVES** yummy shrimp!

"You *did* eat shrimp,"
Mami and Papi say.

"I did," Lola chirps.
"How did you **KNOW?**"

FLAMINGO FACTS

IN THE PiNK

Flamingo chicks hatch with white- or grayish-colored feathers. They are fed pink food from day one. Flamingos feed their young a deep pink drink called "crop milk." Still, chicks' feathers take two to three years to turn pink like their parents'—so a bit longer than Lola's!

FAST FRiENDS

Only five days or so after hatching, the chicks start to explore together. In two to three weeks, these small groups of chicks join each other. Chicks are then kept by an adult or two in very large groups called crèches. It's like preschool for flamingo chicks!

5 FAST FLAMiNGO FACTS

• Flamingos make honking noises like geese.

• The fresh water that flamingos drink can be nearly boiling hot.

• Flamingos are strong swimmers.

• The largest colony of flamingos lives in East Africa, a group of more than 1 million birds.

• Flamingos live for 20 to 30 years in the wild.

Birds of a Feather Feed Together

Flamingos eat foods with red-orange colorings in them and don't typically munch on tropical fruits like Lola does. Some favorite foods are: shrimp, algae, mollusks, small fish, and small insects. These foods stain their feathers pink. When a feather is molted, which means "falls out," the feather loses its pink coloring.

Where, Oh Where?

Six species, or kinds, of flamingos flock all over the world. Whether along warm coastlines or atop cool mountain ranges, flamingos live near shallow, salty waters. That's where they can eat their favorite foods.

Lola is a Chilean flamingo. She lives in South America, where avocados, pepino melons, and dragon fruits grow. Lola's new favorite, pink-staining foods—tiny shrimp, brine flies, and algae—fill South American lakes, lagoons, and wetlands.

For More Flamingo Info

- kids.nationalgeographic.com/animals/flamingo

- justfunfacts.com/interesting-facts-about-flamingos/

- coolkidfacts.com/flamingo-facts-for-kids/

- kidsplayandcreate.com/can-flamingos-fly-flamingo-facts-for-kids

- kids.kiddle.co/Flamingo

- livescience.com/27322-flamingos.html